Overboard!

"Hey!" said Flossie. She pointed to the floor. "Wet tracks. They lead away from Larry's room."

The twins followed the tracks.

"They lead out onto the deck," said Bert. "I don't like this. Come on!"

The twins pulled open the door and went out on the deck.

"Look," said Flossie. "The tracks lead to the railing and stop."

"Oh, no!" cried Freddie. "Larry's jumped!"

Books in The New Bobbsey Twins series

Available from MINSTREL Books

THE NEW
Bobbsey Twins
#6
Twins
MYSTERY ON THE MISSISSIPPI

LAURA LEE HOPE
ILLUSTRATED BY PAUL JENNIS

A MINSTREL® BOOK

PUBLISHED BY POCKET BOOKS

New York   London   Toronto   Sydney   Tokyo

A MINSTREL PAPERBACK *ORIGINAL*

A Minstrel Book published by
POCKET BOOKS, a division of Simon & Schuster Inc.
1230 Avenue of the Americas, New York, N.Y. 10020

Copyright © 1988 by Simon & Schuster Inc.
Cover artwork copyright © 1988 by Linda Thomas
Produced by Mega-Books of New York, Inc.

ISBN: 0-671-62657-4

First Minstrel Books printing June, 1988

10 9 8 7 6 5 4 3 2 1

THE BOBBSEY TWINS, A MINSTREL BOOK and colophon are registered trademarks of Simon & Schuster Inc.

THE NEW BOBBSEY TWINS is a trademark of Simon & Schuster Inc.

Printed in the U.S.A.

Contents

1

All Aboard!

"Five days on a Mississippi riverboat!" said Bert Bobbsey. "This is going to be great!" He leaned over the rail of the *Mississippi Princess* and looked at the mighty Mississippi River flowing below.

Flossie, his younger sister, pointed to her twin brother, Freddie. "Great? I'm stuck with him for five days on this boat. I'd rather stay behind in Davenport, Iowa."

"That's okay with me," Freddie said.

"Come on, guys, we'll have fun together," Nan Bobbsey said. Twelve-year-old Nan was Flossie's and Freddie's older sister and Bert's twin. "We're sailing all the way to New Orleans. And the *Princess* stops in lots of towns along the way. We can go sightseeing and shopping."

Flossie checked her purse. "I still have most of my allowance," she said, grinning at Nan.

"Have you found our cabins yet?" called the twins' father. He and Mrs. Bobbsey were coming up the gangplank.

"Not yet," Bert said. "But the porter told us that they're one flight up, on the Cabin Deck."

"All the staterooms are on that deck," Freddie said. "Come on, follow me." He dashed for the stairs. The rest of the Bobbseys were right behind him.

Suddenly Flossie shouted, "Look!" The Bobbseys looked toward the top of the stairs. A boy in a red plaid shirt and cutoffs dangled upside down from the railing of the Cabin Deck. His bare legs were hooked around the rail. The boy's long blond hair swayed in the breeze. He grinned at the Bobbseys and waved a big straw hat.

"What are you doing?" shouted Mr. Bobbsey.

The boy didn't answer. Instead, he swung himself up onto the deck and disappeared.

"That wasn't very smart," said Mrs. Bobbsey. "He could have fallen."

"Mark Twain would have loved that," Bert

said. "That boy looked and acted just like Huckleberry Finn."

"Who's Mark Twain?" asked Flossie.

"Just about the greatest American writer who ever lived," answered Bert. "He wrote *The Adventures of Tom Sawyer* and *The Adventures of Huckleberry Finn*. I'm reading *Huck Finn* now. It takes place on the Mississippi River— right where we're going."

Flossie headed up the stairs. "Well, right now, I'm going to my cabin. I want to unpack."

A few minutes later, the Bobbseys were in the corridor near their cabins. The three cabins the family had been given were next to each other.

"Nan, let's take A101," Flossie said.

"Bert and I'll take A103, then," Freddie yelled. "That's as far away from Flossie as I can get!"

"Good!" Flossie yelled back.

Mrs. Bobbsey opened the door to A102 and stepped inside. "What a view of the river!" she said, looking out the window.

"Let's look around the boat," Freddie said. "It has four decks, and I want to check out each one!"

"Hold on," Mr. Bobbsey said. "You have bags to unpack."

"Oh, all right," Freddie said with a sigh. He went into his room with Bert.

After they had put their things away, the twins headed upstairs to the Observation Deck.

Nan looked at the passengers bustling around them. "I think this trip is going to be fun!" she said.

"It'll be just like living during the time of Huckleberry Finn," Bert said. "Over a hundred years ago."

"I like living in modern times," Nan said. "They didn't have TV back then."

"They didn't have computers, either," added Freddie. "I would have hated living way back then."

"What about ice cream?" Flossie said. "It would have been *awful* living without ice cream."

"They had ice cream," Bert said. "It was all homemade."

"Excuse me," a sharp voice suddenly said from behind them.

The Bobbseys turned. A tall, handsome man was scowling down at them.

"Have you kids seen Larry Granville?"

The twins shook their heads. "Who's Larry Granville?" asked Bert.

"He's the son of one of the cooks," said the man. "I need to find him." He looked at Bert.

4

"He's about your age. He's wearing cutoff jeans, a red plaid shirt, and a straw hat."

"Oh, the kid who looks like Huck Finn," Bert said. "We were wondering about him."

The man frowned. "Huck is fun to read about," he said. "But a real-life Huck isn't much fun to be around."

Suddenly Freddie's jaw dropped. He had just spotted Larry standing behind the open door of a lounge. The other Bobbseys hadn't noticed him.

Before Freddie could say anything, Larry put his finger to his lips and shook his head slowly. Freddie winked at him. He liked the idea of sharing a secret with Larry.

"Why are you looking for Larry?" asked Nan.

"That little thief stole something from me," the man said. "I need to find him and make him give it back."

Freddie looked over at the door where Larry had been standing. But Larry was gone.

"We saw him about a half hour ago," said Freddie. He started to laugh, then stopped himself quickly.

The man gave him a funny look.

"He was hanging over the rail on the Cabin Deck," said Flossie.

"Well, if you see him again, please let me know," the man said. "It's very important." He turned to leave.

Nan stopped him. "Are you taking the boat all the way to New Orleans, Mr.—?"

"Ford. Barton Ford. I'm a writer. Larry took a page of my notes for the book I'm writing. And, yes, I'm going all the way to New Orleans, Miss—um—"

"I'm Nan Bobbsey," Nan said. "This is my sister, Flossie, and our brothers, Bert and Freddie."

Flossie gave Mr. Ford a big smile. "We're twins," she said. The breeze ruffled her golden curls.

Mr. Ford smiled back at her. "I can see that," he said.

"What's your book about?" asked Nan.

"Mark Twain and the characters in his books," said Mr. Ford. "Especially Tom Sawyer and Huck Finn."

"Wow," Bert said. "I like Mark Twain, too. He's one of my favorite writers."

Mr. Ford frowned. Bert was puzzled. He wondered if he'd said something wrong. Then he realized Mr. Ford was looking at something behind him. Bert turned to see what Mr. Ford was staring at.

"There he is!" cried Mr. Ford.

Larry was hanging over the rail again, behind the Bobbseys.

Mr. Ford glared at him. "You thief!" he shouted, rushing toward Larry. "Give me back my notes!"

Larry tried to swing up onto the deck, but he moved too quickly and lost his grip. His leg slipped.

"He's falling," Flossie screamed. "Right into the river!"

2

Pirate Gold

Larry twisted in the air and grabbed onto one of the rail posts. His fingers slid down the post, slowing his fall. Then he dropped onto the deck below and took off, running.

Mr. Ford charged down the stairs after him. The Bobbseys watched the two of them disappear around a corner.

"This may turn out to be an even more exciting trip than I thought," said Bert.

Just then, a loud whistle blew. White smoke puffed from the stacks of the *Mississippi Princess.*

"We're about to get going," said Freddie. He hurried to the rail, followed by Bert and Flossie.

"Look at that huge paddle wheel!" Flossie said. "It's turning."

"I can't believe we're on a brand-new steamboat headed down the Mississippi," said Bert. He turned to Nan. "Aren't you going to watch?"

"I'm wondering about Larry and Mr. Ford," Nan said thoughtfully.

"I don't think Larry's a thief," said Freddie.

"Maybe, maybe not," Bert said. "Come on, let's go look around."

The next morning the Bobbsey family was up early. "Breakfast first," Mr. Bobbsey said, leading the way to the ship's coffee shop. "Afterward, I'll conduct you on a guided tour."

For several hours, the Bobbseys wandered around the four levels of the ship. The outside looked like an old-style riverboat, but the inside was modern. There were two swimming pools, a movie theater, and a library.

"Wow," Bert said as they stood in the library just before lunchtime. "Look in this display case. There's a copy of *The Adventures of Huckleberry Finn*. And it's autographed by Mark Twain!"

"Isn't that wonderful?" said Mrs. Bobbsey.

"Lunch would *really* be wonderful," Flossie said. "I'm hungry again!"

The Bobbseys headed for the Orleans Room,

one of the two fancy restaurants on the ship. There were oil lamps on the tables and mirrors in the ceiling. And the food was great.

That afternoon, Mr. and Mrs. Bobbsey went for a swim in the outdoor pool. The twins were on the Sun Deck, at the top of the boat.

"What are they doing in there?" Flossie asked. She pointed at the crew members behind a big window.

"That's the wheelhouse," Bert explained. "The captain and the crew steer the boat from there."

"Look at those guys fishing on the shore," Freddie said, shielding his eyes from the sun. "I wonder if they're catching anything."

"I want to go to the gift shop," Flossie said. "But I'd better count my money first." She opened her purse and felt around inside. Her fingers touched something damp—something that shouldn't have been there.

Flossie pulled the thing out. When she saw what it was, she dropped it and screamed. A dead fish!

"Yuck," said Bert. He picked up the fish and tossed it overboard.

"Who would do something dumb like that?" Nan asked.

"Don't ask me," Flossie said. "I put my purse down for a minute while we—"

"Hey, look down there!" Freddie interrupted. He waved and yelled, "Hi!"

Larry was sitting on the rail below them. "Hi!" he shouted back.

"Did you put that fish inside my purse?" Flossie demanded.

"Maybe I did and maybe I didn't," said Larry. He jumped off the rail and ran upstairs to them.

"You almost broke your neck yesterday, falling off that other rail," Nan told him.

Larry shrugged. "That fall didn't hurt me," he said. "I'm tough."

"You didn't answer me," said Flossie. She glared at Larry. "That fish was disgusting."

Bert grinned, and Freddie started to laugh.

Nan frowned at her brothers. "It's not funny," she said.

"Right," Bert said, still grinning.

"But it sure made Flossie scream," Freddie said with a hoot of laughter.

"I wasn't scared," Flossie said. Then she sniffed at her purse. "Yuck! What a smell!" She waved her purse around to try to air it out.

"It was *supposed* to be a joke," said Larry. He had a big grin on his face.

"Do you always do stuff like that?" asked Freddie. "Play jokes on people, I mean."

"Sometimes," Larry said. "There's nothing else to do on this stupid boat." He looked around. "So, where's your friend Barton Ford?"

"He's not our friend," Flossie said. "We only just met him."

"He's writing a book," Nan said. "It's all about Mark Twain and the characters in his books. You know, Tom Sawyer and Huckleberry Finn."

"He doesn't know anything about Mark Twain or Tom Sawyer—or even Huck Finn," Larry scoffed.

"And I suppose you do?" asked Bert.

Larry nodded. "I've read *Huckleberry Finn* twenty-seven times." He grinned at them. "I'm reading it again now, so that'll make twenty-eight."

Freddie's eyes widened. "Wow, you must really like that book."

"Does your father always let you go with him on the steamboat?" asked Nan.

"Yeah," answered Larry. "But the only reason he does is because he wants me to tell him where my mother buried a pirate's treasure chest before she died."

The twins looked at each other. "We're sorry about your mother," Nan said gently to Larry. "But that stuff about buried pirate treasure—are you sure you didn't just make that up?"

"I don't make things up," insisted Larry. "I always tell the truth."

"What about Mr. Ford's notes for his book?" Bert asked. "Did you steal them?"

"No," Larry said with a frown.

"I thought you always told the truth," said Bert.

"I do," said Larry.

"Mr. Ford said you took them," Nan insisted.

"I didn't *steal* them," said Larry. He looked at the twins. "I just *borrowed* them."

"Could we see them?" asked Bert.

Larry shrugged. "Sure," he said. He took a folded paper out of his back pocket. "But they don't make any sense. See for yourself."

Nan took the paper and looked at it carefully. "This is really strange," she said, shaking her head.

"What is?" asked Flossie, glancing at the paper.

"This paper just has a lot of numbers and letters on it," said Nan. "50,000 AUTO. AHF . . . I can't figure it out, either." She folded up the paper and handed it back to Larry.

"What did I tell you?" said Larry. He put the paper back in his pocket.

"You still had no right to take that," Nan

said. "It doesn't belong to you."

"I'll give it back—one of these days," Larry said. "Just as soon as Barton Ford apologizes for the names he called me."

"Tell us about that buried treasure," Flossie said. "That sounds exciting. If it's real."

"It's real, all right," Larry said. "My mother found some pirate's gold down in New Orleans. She buried it in a cave under one of the bluffs along the river. And," he added, "I'm the only person who knows where it is."

"Are you sure you're not making this up?" Bert asked.

"Nope," insisted Larry. "Maybe I'll be able to show you a few coins before we get to New Orleans. I might even tell you where the cave is."

"That would be great!" exclaimed Freddie.

"I said 'maybe.' "

"Larry!" An angry-looking man in a white uniform was hurrying down the deck toward Larry and the twins.

"It's my dad," muttered Larry. He turned and started to walk away.

Mr. Granville rushed up to Larry and grabbed him by the shoulder.

"You're supposed to be in your room doing your schoolwork," Mr. Granville said sternly. "What are you doing out here?"

"Just talking, Dad," Larry said.

"Well, quit your talking and get back to the cabin," Mr. Granville said. "I've got to get back to work." He ran down the stairs toward one of the restaurants on the Observation Deck.

Larry didn't move. Instead, he leaned against the rail and stared out at the river.

"Shouldn't you do what he says?" Nan asked him.

Larry turned to her. "I'll go when I'm good and ready," he said. "I don't like being told what to do all the time."

"Just like Huck Finn," Bert muttered under his breath.

Just then the door to the wheelhouse opened.

"Here comes Captain Collins," Freddie said. "He looks mad. And Mr. Ford's with him."

Larry started to run toward the stairs.

"Larry!" Captain Collins shouted. "Hold it right there!"

Larry stopped and turned around. "Yes, sir?" he said. "Is something wrong?"

"I think you know what's wrong," said Mr. Ford. He turned to the twins.

"First, he steals my notes. Now a valuable book is missing from the ship's library. It's been stolen. And we know who did it!"

3

Larry in Trouble

"What book is missing?" asked Bert.

"The autographed copy of Mark Twain's *The Adventures of Huckleberry Finn,*" Captain Collins said. "It's one of the ship's most prized possessions. And, as Mr. Ford said, it's very valuable."

"It's worth at least $50,000," Mr. Ford put in. "I've been using it for research for my book."

"I didn't steal it," Larry insisted.

"And I suppose you didn't take my notes, either," Mr. Ford said.

"Oh, all right," Larry said. "So I took that dumb old piece of paper. So what?"

"I knew it!" Mr. Ford said. He glared at

Larry. "You'd better give it back to me—right now!"

"Well, I'd like to," Larry said, looking innocently at Mr. Ford. "But I can't remember where I put it."

The twins looked at each other. They wanted to defend Larry, but they didn't know what to say. He had lied about the paper. Was he lying about stealing the book, too?

Captain Collins set his jaw. "Well, maybe you can remember where you put *this!*" He took out a pocketknife and showed it to Larry. "Do you recognize it?" he asked.

Larry nodded. "That's my knife," he said. "Where'd you find it?"

"In the library, right next to the display case of rare books," said Captain Collins. "The lock had been pried open."

"Oh, no," Freddie said with a groan.

"You used the knife to pry open the lock," Mr. Ford said accusingly.

"I didn't!" Larry said. "You've got to believe me!"

"Then how did your knife get by the display case? You must have dropped it there," said Captain Collins.

"I don't know how it got there," Larry said desperately.

Mr. Granville rushed up to them. "What's

this about your stealing that book?" he asked his son.

"I didn't do it, Dad," Larry said. "But nobody believes me."

Mr. Granville looked at Captain Collins. "What happened?" he asked.

Captain Collins described the theft. "We found Larry's knife by the display case in the library," he finished.

Mr. Granville's eyes narrowed as he looked at his son. His voice became hard and low. "I've told you again and again not to take things that don't belong to you."

"But I didn't—not this time," Larry said. "Why would I want to steal a dumb old book, anyway?"

Captain Collins put his hand on Larry's shoulder. "Look, Larry," he said. "A couple of weeks ago, you took a valuable book from my office. It was part of my personal rare-book collection."

"But I gave it right back! It was only a joke."

"I know," Captain Collins said. "But now another valuable book is missing. Everything points to you as the thief."

Nan glanced at Freddie. He was shaking his head sadly.

"Go to the cabin, Larry," Mr. Granville said.

"I'll see you there in a few minutes. It's time you and I had a long talk."

Larry started to say something, but his father's stern look stopped him. He shrugged and walked off toward the Cabin Deck.

"Mr. Granville," Captain Collins said, "we'd like to search your cabin. If you don't mind." Mr. Granville nodded. "And," the captain continued, "you're going to have to do something about Larry."

"You have my word that Larry won't cause you any more trouble," Mr. Granville said firmly. He turned and left.

"It doesn't look too good for Larry," Bert whispered to Nan.

"I know what you mean," she said. "He's played so many jokes on people that no one believes anything he says anymore."

"This is turning out to be some research trip," said Mr. Ford. "If we don't find that missing book, I'll never get my work done. As it is, I can only use it at night after the library has closed."

"We'll help you look for it," offered Bert.

"It's got to be somewhere on the boat," added Nan.

"Right," said Freddie.

"Well, we can use all the help we can get,"

Captain Collins said with a sigh. "Right now I have to radio the president of the steamship company. And the police. They'll meet us in Burlington, our next stop." He shook his head. "I really don't know how I'm going to explain this to the Hannibal Historical Society." With that, he left the deck, followed by Mr. Ford.

"I'm beginning to feel sorry for Larry," Nan said. "He looked as if he was telling the truth— for a change."

"But he did take a book from Captain Collins's collection," said Bert. "And he lied about the paper. That makes him look pretty guilty to me."

"He looks *too* guilty," Nan said. "Besides, it's odd that Captain Collins also collects rare books."

"I'll bet he's the one who stole it," Freddie said. "It's probably in his office with the other rare books."

"No, anybody might see it there," Nan said. "If he took it, he probably hid it somewhere else on the boat."

"But where?" asked Flossie.

"Well, we could just start looking around," suggested Nan, "and see what we come up with."

"I say we start looking in the lounges," said Bert.

The other twins agreed. For the next two hours, they searched the steamboat. They even looked in the lifeboats.

"No luck," Bert said. "Whoever stole the book hid it very carefully."

"I'm hungry," said Flossie.

Freddie grinned at her. "So what else is new," he said teasingly.

Flossie made a face at her brother.

Bert looked at his watch. "No wonder you're hungry. It's almost time to meet Mom and Dad for dinner."

The twins found their way to the Orleans Room. Mr. and Mrs. Bobbsey were already seated at a table in front of the band.

Mr. Bobbsey raised an eyebrow as the twins sat down. "I hope you children brought your appetites," he said, looking around the restaurant. "The food looks wonderful."

"It sure does," said Flossie, eyeing the dessert table a few feet away from them.

The waiter took their orders. Then Mrs. Bobbsey said, "I hear your friend Larry Granville is in trouble."

"How'd you know that?" asked Flossie.

"Everyone on the boat is talking about it," said Mr. Bobbsey. "He's been accused of stealing a valuable book."

Nan took a sip of water. "Well, we

don't think he stole anything," she said.

"You must be the only ones," said Mr. Bobbsey. "Everybody else thinks he did."

"He's really not a bad kid," Bert said as he buttered a roll.

"He just likes to borrow things," said Freddie.

"Things that don't belong to him," said Mr. Bobbsey.

"But he always gives everything back," Freddie protested.

"And he'd be the perfect one to blame if someone else was the thief," Nan pointed out.

Soon the waiter served their dinner. As they ate they began talking about what they planned to do in New Orleans.

They had just finished dessert when Freddie spotted Mr. Granville.

"Hey," said Freddie. He grabbed Bert's arm. "I just saw Larry's father go through that swinging door."

"That's the galley, the ship's kitchen," Bert explained.

"Maybe we should talk to him." Nan turned to their parents. "Could we, Mom? Dad? Just to see how Larry is doing."

Mr. and Mrs. Bobbsey exchanged glances. They knew it was hard to stop the twins when they were hot on a trail.

"All right," Mr. Bobbsey said. "But try not to interrupt his work."

The twins thanked their parents and got up.

In the galley, they found Mr. Granville setting a plate of food on a tray.

"Hi, Mr. Granville," Bert said. "We just wanted to ask how Larry was doing."

"You're not allowed in the galley," Mr. Granville said. Then his expression softened. "But you kids could do me a big favor."

"What is it?" Nan asked.

"I'm too busy to leave the galley. Would you take Larry's dinner to him? I have it right here on this tray. He's in cabin H337."

"Sure," Bert said. He grabbed the tray and led the others out of the galley.

"Now we can question Larry on our own. And we might just—"

"Pick up some clues!" Freddie cried.

Bert smiled.

When the twins arrived at room H337, they found the door unlocked.

Bert pushed the door open. "Larry!" he called.

Freddie stuck his head inside the room. "There's nobody here," he said.

"Hey!" said Flossie. She pointed to the floor. The twins looked down and saw wet tracks leading away from the room.

Bert quickly put the tray of food down on a table. Then he and the other twins began to follow the tracks.

"They lead out onto the deck," said Bert. "I don't like this. Come on!"

The twins pulled open the door and went out on deck.

"Look," said Flossie. "The tracks lead to the railing and stop."

"Oh, no!" cried Freddie. "Larry's jumped!"

4

Boy Overboard!

Freddie ran up the stairs and raced back along the corridor. He pushed open the galley door. "Larry's jumped overboard!" he shouted from the doorway.

"We saw his tracks," Flossie said, coming up behind Freddie. "Outside his room."

Mr. Granville turned white. In the dining room, Captain Collins stood up. His table was near the galley, and he had heard what Freddie and Flossie had said. Several passengers at his table got up, too.

Mr. Granville rushed out of the dining room and down to the Cabin Deck. The twins followed. Barton Ford and Captain Collins were right behind them, along with members of the crew.

"Go check those tracks," the captain told a crew member. Then he shouted, "Stop the ship!" into an intercom on the wall. "Shine the searchlights on the river!"

"I can't believe he'd do a thing like this," said Mr. Granville. His eyes searched the river. The *Mississippi Princess* shuddered, then stopped.

Flossie watched Mr. Granville. "Now he can get Larry's mother's buried treasure," she whispered to Freddie.

"Not without Larry," Freddie whispered back. "He was the only one who knew where it was, remember?"

The crew member who had gone to Larry's cabin came back. He spoke to Captain Collins and pointed at the river. The captain nodded. "Starboard side aft," he yelled into the intercom. The lights played on the river at the rear of the boat.

Mr. Ford was leaning over the rail, staring at the river. "Now I'll never get my notes back."

"Mr. Ford!" Nan said. "Larry may have drowned!"

"I'm sorry if something has happened to him," said Mr. Ford. He looked embarrassed. "But I need those notes for my book!"

"I don't know why they're so important," Nan said. "They looked like a bunch of nonsense numbers and letters to me."

Mr. Ford stared at Nan. For a moment, there was a strange look on his face. Then he turned away.

Groups of passengers began to line the rail.

"Lower the lifeboats!" shouted Captain Collins above the noise of the crowd. Then he headed for the wheelhouse on the Sun Deck.

"What are they doing now?" asked Flossie.

"They can get a better look if they're in the water," said Freddie.

"There you are!" Mr. Bobbsey called, hurrying to the twins.

"It's just terrible about Larry," said Mrs. Bobbsey.

"Maybe not," said Bert.

Nan and the twins looked at him.

"What do you mean?" asked Mrs. Bobbsey.

"I was just thinking about something," Bert said. "Mom? Dad? Could we go inside?"

Mr. and Mrs. Bobbsey nodded. "We'll be here if you need us," Mrs. Bobbsey said.

In the corridor, away from the crowd, Bert said, "You know, it just hit me. Those tracks are kind of suspicious."

"What are you talking about?" asked Flossie. "We all saw the tracks—and where they led."

"But why are there footprints at all?" Bert asked. "Especially *wet* tracks leading *away* from Larry's cabin."

"Right!" said Freddie, his eyes lighting up. "Larry's feet wouldn't be wet *before* he jumped into the water."

"One of Larry's pranks!" said Nan.

"Of course!" Flossie said. "Why didn't I think of that?" She slapped her hand to her forehead.

"The more I think about it," Bert said, "the more I know Larry wouldn't jump overboard. But he might try to make everyone *think* he had."

"Then where is he?" asked Nan.

"I don't know," Bert said. "We'll just have to search the entire steamboat."

The twins started with the Sun Deck and began working their way down. They looked in the lounges and the empty theater. They even tried the two swimming pools. But there was no sign of Larry.

"I need to stop in our cabin for a few minutes," Flossie said when they'd reached the Cabin Deck. She opened her purse and began rummaging through it. "I can't find my key."

"Here. Use mine," Nan said, handing Flossie her key.

"Hurry up," Bert said. "We'll wait out here."

Flossie unlocked the door, stepped inside the cabin, and turned on the light. "I just want to get my—" She stopped short and stared at the window. Then she let out a scream.

Bert, Nan, and Freddie rushed into the cabin.

"What is it, Flossie?" Nan asked. "What's wrong?"

Flossie raised her arm slowly and pointed. Two feet were sticking out at the bottom of the window curtain.

"All right, you, come on out!" shouted Bert.

But whoever was behind the curtain didn't move.

Bert marched over to the curtain and grabbed it.

"Oh, Bert, be careful!" whispered Flossie.

The curtain slowly parted.

"Larry!" Freddie shouted.

"Not so loud," Larry said. "Somebody'll hear you!"

"Captain Collins is going to be really mad at you now," said Bert.

"Everybody is looking for you," Freddie said. "They think you drowned."

"That's what I want them to think," Larry said. "Otherwise they'll put me in jail!"

"You've got to give yourself up," Nan said. "Or everybody will think you really are the thief."

"He *is* a thief," Flossie said. "I'll bet he took the key from my purse."

Larry nodded. "I did it for fun," he said. "Then when I needed a place to hide, I used it." He handed the key to Flossie. "I'm sorry." He looked at Bert. For the first time, Larry looked helpless. "I guess I'm really in trouble."

"You sure are!" Bert said. "But we want to help you."

Nan stepped closer to Larry. "We're pretty good at solving mysteries."

"That's right," said Freddie.

"Everybody's heard of us back in Lakeport," added Flossie. "That's where we're from."

"Really?" Larry said. "Okay, I'll turn myself in. But only if you promise to prove I'm not guilty."

"We'll need your help, too," Nan said.

"You've got it," said Larry.

"Then come on," Bert said. "Let's go find Captain Collins."

The twins and Larry went up to the Sun Deck where Captain Collins was still directing the search.

"Captain! We found Larry," Bert called.

"What!" Captain Collins turned around. When he saw Larry, his face grew hard.

"Clear the deck!" he ordered. "Mr. Granville, I have a few things to say to you and your son right now." He turned to the Bobbseys. "You kids, too!"

When the others had left the deck, Larry explained why he wanted everyone to think he had jumped overboard. Captain Collins listened in silence until Larry had finished. Then he looked at Larry sternly. "I'll be as clear about this as I know how," the captain said. "No more tricks, no more jokes—or your father loses his job!"

Larry and his father looked at each other.

"You know the way to your cabin, son," Mr. Granville said. "I still have work to do in the galley." They went below deck.

Captain Collins turned to the twins. "And you four should be choosier about your friends," he said. "Larry Granville's walking a thin line. And you will be, too, if you're not careful. Now good night."

The twins left and headed for their cabins.

"Why was he mad at us?" asked Freddie.

"He probably thinks we helped Larry plan the whole thing tonight," Nan grumbled.

"What are we going to do now?" Flossie asked.

Bert sighed. "I don't know. But we'd better think of something. And fast."

5

First Port of Call

At nine the next morning, the *Mississippi Princess* docked at her first port of call, Burlington, Iowa.

"What's wrong?" Mrs. Bobbsey asked the twins at breakfast. "You all have dark circles under your eyes."

"I didn't sleep too well," said Nan.

"Me, neither," said Freddie.

"Look," said Bert, pointing to the door.

Two police officers had come into the dining room. They looked around, then left.

"Excuse us," Flossie said as she stood up.

"Sit back down, please," said Mr. Bobbsey. He had a frown on his face.

"But, Dad," Bert said, "didn't you see those police officers? They're probably here to talk to Larry!"

"It can wait," Mrs. Bobbsey said. "Finish your breakfast first."

"That was a stupid prank Larry pulled last night," Mr. Bobbsey said. "That boy seems to attract trouble. I expect you kids to be careful."

"That's just what Captain Collins told us last night," Nan said with a sigh.

The twins finished eating. Finally, they excused themselves and rushed off to Larry's room.

They found the police officers talking to Mr. Granville. Captain Collins and Barton Ford were in the room, too.

The twins stood quietly outside the door and listened as Captain Collins finished describing the stolen book to the officers.

"Besides that," Mr. Ford added, "Larry has stolen a piece of paper from me. It contains some very important notes."

One of the police officers looked at Mr. Granville. "This is all very serious, sir," he said. "Would you and your son come to the station? We need to ask you both some questions."

"What's going to happen, Dad?" cried Larry.

Mr. Granville shook his head. "I don't know," he said.

"Bert, we promised Larry we'd help him," whispered Flossie. "Let's do something!"

"I know, Floss. But Larry has played dirty tricks on people. And he's lied. He's even stolen things. I don't know if we can help him. I don't know if anyone can."

The Bobbseys stood aside to let Larry, Mr. Granville, and the police officers leave the room.

"What are you doing here?" Captain Collins asked when he saw the Bobbseys.

"We came to see if we could help Larry," said Bert.

"We promised him," Flossie added. She gave the captain a big smile. The captain didn't smile back.

"It's too late," said Mr. Ford, shaking his head. "It's a police matter now."

Just then, two more police officers arrived. "Do we have your permission to search the *Mississippi Princess?*" the woman officer asked the captain.

"You most certainly do," said Captain Collins. "My entire crew is at your disposal. We have to find that book. It doesn't belong to the steamship company. And it's worth a lot of money."

"We'll be glad to help you," Freddie said to the officer.

She looked down at him and smiled. "Thanks," she said. "Maybe next time."

Captain Collins began walking down the corridor with the two police officers.

The twins followed them, staying far enough behind so they wouldn't be seen.

The captain led the police officers to the library and showed them the display case.

"The rare book was in here," said Captain Collins. "As you can see, the lock has been broken."

"We'll check the case for fingerprints," the male officer said. He opened a black bag and took out powder and a brush.

At a signal from Bert, the twins stepped into the library.

"Need any help?" Bert asked.

"I told you kids not to interfere," said Captain Collins.

Bert shrugged. "Just thought I'd ask," he said.

The twins pretended to look for books to read. But they watched every move the police officers made.

Finally, the male officer said, "I got lots of prints off the case. But they're all different."

"Several passengers looked at the display," said Captain Collins. "The fingerprints could belong to anybody, I guess."

"You're right," said the officer. "I thought I had a good one down here, next to the broken lock. But it's smudged."

Bert walked over for a closer look. But Captain Collins frowned at him.

"We were just leaving," Nan said quickly. She put her book back on the shelf. "Come on," she said to the others.

They left the library.

"Found anything yet?"

The twins turned around. Mr. Ford was smiling at them.

"Not yet," Bert said. "Why?"

"I was just wondering, that's all," said Mr. Ford. He turned and walked away.

"What are we going to do now?" asked Freddie.

"What we always do," Bert answered. "Look for clues."

"We've looked already," said Flossie. "There aren't any."

"Don't give up the ship," said Bert. He gave Flossie a smile. "We'll just have to keep looking."

The twins were on deck after lunch when a police car arrived at the dock. Larry and his father got out of the car.

"Look!" shouted Flossie.

"Larry!" called Freddie. He began to wave. But Larry kept his head down.

"Let's go to his cabin and wait for him," suggested Nan.

The twins hurried to the Cabin Deck. A few minutes later, Mr. Granville and Larry arrived at their cabin.

"May we talk to Larry?" asked Nan.

"No, you may not!" snapped Mr. Granville. He unlocked the cabin door and pushed Larry into the room. Then he closed the door—and locked it.

"What happened at the police station?" asked Bert.

"Larry has to be back in Burlington in eight days," Mr. Granville said. "The police want to question him some more. In the meantime, the *Princess* will be allowed to continue on down the river. All I can say is, thank goodness I won't lose my job." He hurried away down the corridor.

"That's all he thinks about," Flossie said. "His job!"

"Right," Freddie said. "But I'm glad that Larry didn't have to spend the night in jail."

"So am I," Bert said, nodding.

"But he's locked in his room," Nan said. "That's almost as bad."

Flossie knelt at the keyhole. "Don't worry,

Larry. The Bobbseys are on the job," she shouted.

"Leave me alone," Larry shouted back. "Go away."

"Come on," Bert said. "We'll talk to him later."

After dinner, the twins went out on the Sun Deck.

"Maybe we should go down to Larry's room and try to talk to him again," said Freddie.

"No," Nan said. "We'd just get him into more trouble. And we might get ourselves in trouble, too." She stared at the river. "What we've got to do is start thinking out this case."

"As I see it, we've got two suspects," Bert said. "Captain Collins and Barton Ford."

Nan nodded. "Both of them had reasons for taking that book. Captain Collins could have wanted it for his collection. Barton Ford for the book he's writing."

"Well, I think it's Mr. Granville," said Flossie.

"Why?" said Freddie, staring at his sister.

"Because if Larry has to go to jail, then Mr. Granville will get the buried treasure!"

Freddie rolled his eyes. "How many times do I have to tell you? Larry's the only one who knows where it is!"

Flossie tossed her head. "Well, Mr. Granville will *make* Larry tell him where it is before he goes to jail."

"Come on, you guys, I'm sure Larry made up that story about a buried treasure," said Nan.

"I think it's the truth," said Flossie.

Just then, Captain Collins came out of the wheelhouse. He headed down the deck away from them. He was carrying a screwdriver and a few other tools.

"What's he doing?" asked Flossie.

"I don't know," Bert said. "But I think we should find out."

Captain Collins went down two flights of stairs to the Cabin Deck. He was muttering to himself. "I'll fix 'em for good!" he said just loud enough for the twins to hear. "If you want something done right, you've got to do it yourself!" Then he turned a corner and disappeared from view.

"Did you hear what he said?" whispered Nan.

"I sure did," said Bert. "Come on!"

The twins peeked around the corner but Captain Collins was nowhere in sight. They crept along the deck, looking for him.

Finally, the twins reached the railings above the paddle wheel. The huge wheel was turning

slowly. Each of its blades looked like giant slats. They pushed downward and through the water, causing the boat to move—and the river to churn below.

"He's gone," said Nan. She had to shout to be heard over the noise.

"What was he doing with those tools?" yelled Bert.

"Maybe he's building something," Freddie shouted.

"Or hiding the book," yelled Bert.

Behind them, Flossie stood on tiptoe to get a better look at the paddle wheel. Then she leaned against the railing. The wood began to creak, but she couldn't hear it above the noise. Suddenly the wood cracked loudly. And the rail broke.

"Help!" Flossie screamed. She felt herself going over, tumbling toward the huge, churning paddles.

6
Larry Disappears— Again

"Flossie!" Nan whirled around and grabbed for her sister.

But Bert was faster. He caught Flossie's hand just in time and pulled her back. They both fell to the deck with a loud thud.

The broken railing bounced off the paddle wheel and plunged into the water below.

"Flossie! Are you okay?" Freddie cried.

Flossie hugged herself, trembling. She nodded. "I—I'm okay," she said shakily.

Nan looked at the rail. "No wonder Captain Collins was carrying those tools!" she said. "He was probably taking the rail apart!"

"What for?" Bert asked.

"I don't know. But he's a suspect, isn't he?" said Nan.

"What are you kids doing here?"

The twins looked up. Captain Collins was standing over them holding a sign.

"Flossie almost fell into the paddle wheel," said Bert.

"Oh, no!" The captain looked at Flossie closely. "You didn't get hurt, did you?"

"No," Flossie said. "No thanks to you!"

"What do you mean, 'no thanks' to me?" Captain Collins asked in a surprised tone.

"We saw you with those tools," Freddie said. "We know what you were doing."

"I'm sorry I didn't get back here soon enough," said the captain. "But I can't do everything myself."

"What are you talking about?" Nan asked in a puzzled voice.

Captain Collins held up the sign. It read: DANGER! BROKEN RAILING!

"They were supposed to repair this while we were in port," he said. "But one of the crew just told me it still felt loose, so I came to check it myself. When I saw it still needed work, I went to get this sign. Now I'll have to rope off this area."

He found a rope and began to tie it and the sign across the broken section.

"Too bad that sign wasn't there before," said Flossie. She still felt shaky as the twins left the paddle-wheel area and walked toward their cabins.

"I think we all need to go to bed," said Nan. "We can wait until morning to tell Mom and Dad what happened."

"Right," Bert said. "This has been a rough day."

"See you tomorrow," Nan said. She put her arm around Flossie and led her into their cabin.

"Bert," Freddie said as they headed to their cabin, "do you think Captain Collins was telling the truth about that rail?"

"I don't know," Bert said. "Why would he want to loosen the rail? It really doesn't make sense."

Early the next morning, the *Mississippi Princess* docked in Hannibal, Missouri.

"This is going to be an exciting day," Mr. Bobbsey said at breakfast. "Hannibal is Mark Twain's hometown."

Mrs. Bobbsey pointed to the window. "Look over there. See those two little islands in the middle of the river? I'll bet they'd make a great hiding place for a character in a mystery."

The twins didn't say anything. Mr. and Mrs. Bobbsey looked at each other.

"You're the one who talked us into taking this trip, Bert," Mr. Bobbsey said. "You could try to be a little excited about it."

"Sorry, Dad," Bert said. Then he told his parents about Flossie's accident.

"How awful! You could have been killed," said Mrs. Bobbsey, hugging Flossie to her.

Flossie's eyes grew wide. "It was—" she began.

"Look!" Nan said suddenly.

Mr. Granville had come running into the Orleans Room. He rushed over and whispered something into Captain Collins's ear.

The captain turned red. He threw down his fork and hurried out of the dining room.

"I bet Larry's in trouble again," said Freddie.

"He can't seem to stay out of it, can he?" said Mrs. Bobbsey, her arm still around Flossie.

Bert stood up, but Mr. Bobbsey looked at him with raised eyebrows. Bert sat back down.

The twins finished eating. Then they rushed up to Larry's room.

Captain Collins and Mr. Granville were standing in the doorway. Mr. Ford was with them.

"What happened?" asked Bert.

"I forgot to lock the door this morning!" said Mr. Granville. "Larry's gone!"

"He must have left the ship right after we

docked," said Captain Collins. "I'll have to send out a search party to find him—even it it holds us up."

The captain stepped into the hall and spoke into the intercom. "Attention all passengers," he said. "We'll be in Hannibal longer than expected, waiting for special cargo. If you go ashore, please listen for the ship's whistle. It will sound one hour before we sail. Thank you." He turned off the intercom and muttered, "Special cargo named Larry Granville."

The twins went back to the Orleans Room. Most of the passengers were excited about the holdover. They seemed glad to have the chance to spend extra time in Mark Twain's hometown.

The twins told their parents that Larry had disappeared again.

"What do you four plan to do?" asked Mrs. Bobbsey.

"We're going to look for him," said Bert.

"Are you going to spend the whole trip looking for Larry Granville?" asked Mr. Bobbsey.

"He's been accused of something he didn't do," Nan said. "We promised to help him. Anyway," she added, "we can do some sightseeing while we're looking for him."

"Well, since Hannibal's a small town, I guess

it's all right," Mr. Bobbsey said. "Just don't go too far from the steamboat."

A few minutes later, the twins raced down the gangplank behind Captain Collins's search party.

"Where are we going first?" asked Flossie.

"There's no point in following the search party," Nan said. "We should look in a different direction. That way, the whole town will be covered."

Bert nodded. "I thought we'd check out the churches," he said. "Huck Finn once showed up at a church after he ran away. Everyone thought he'd drowned. They were holding funeral services for him!"

"That's cool," Freddie said. "Let's go."

But after several hours of looking inside churches, the twins still hadn't found Larry.

At three o'clock, they found a coffee shop and had lunch. When they left, Freddie said, "There's another church over there."

An old wooden church stood at the side of the road. A graveyard stretched behind it, ending at a bluff facing the river.

"Let's give it a try," said Bert.

The church was empty and dark. The only light came from the tall, narrow windows.

"He's probably hiding in one of the pews or up front somewhere," said Freddie.

"*If* he's in here," Flossie said.

They started down the center aisle, but stopped in their tracks. Somewhere behind them, a door had squeaked.

"What was that?" asked Flossie. She moved closer to Nan.

"Maybe it's Larry," said Nan.

"And maybe it's not," Bert said.

The twins turned around slowly. A small, bent figure appeared at the rear of the church. It began to walk toward them.

Nan gulped. "Let's get out of here."

She turned abruptly and bumped into a man behind her. She screamed.

"It's all right," the man said. "I didn't mean to frighten you."

Nan's heart was almost in her throat. "We've got to get out of here," she managed to say. "There's somebody after us!"

"It's just Old Ben," the man said. "Ben," he shouted at the bent figure, "it's all right. I'll take care of things. You can go back to work."

Old Ben turned and walked toward a side door at the rear of the church.

"I'm Pastor Vary," the man said. "This is my church. Is there something I can do for you?"

"We're looking for a friend of ours," said Bert.

"His name is Larry," Nan said. "He ran away

from our ship this morning. We're from the *Mississippi Princess*."

"We have to find him," said Flossie.

"He's in a lot of trouble," Freddie added.

"Slow down, slow down," Pastor Vary said with a smile. "I think I heard about the lost boy. Seems like everybody's looking for him."

"But we have to find him first," said Bert.

Pastor Vary raised his eyebrows. "Why are you looking here?" he asked.

"Larry acts like Huck Finn," Nan said. "Huck Finn went to a church once when he ran away."

Pastor Vary smiled. "Well, I haven't seen your friend," he said. "And I've been here all day. But there are other churches in town. You might try those."

"We have!" Freddie said with a groan.

"Thank you, anyway," said Bert.

The twins left the church and turned the corner.

"Wait!" The voice came from behind them.

They stopped and looked around. Nobody was there.

"Wait!" the voice called again.

Old Ben stepped out from behind some bushes.

"What's . . . what's wrong?" Bert managed to say.

"Are you looking for Huck Finn?" Old Ben asked in a raspy voice.

"Uh, well, sort of," said Bert.

"I saw his ghost this morning," Old Ben said. "Very early. Would have known him anywhere."

"Do you know where he went?" asked Nan.

Old Ben smiled at the twins. "Oh, yes," he said softly. "I know where he went. I followed him." He started laughing.

Flossie clung tightly to Bert.

"Where'd he go?" asked Freddie.

"To the cemetery," Old Ben said, pointing behind the church. "I followed him there. He went back to his grave."

7

Grave Business

"Oh . . . well, thanks for the information," said Nan. She looked at the other twins. "Uh, we'd better be going, don't you think?"

The twins edged away from Old Ben.

"That's right," Bert said with a nod. "We need to keep looking for . . . uh, Huck Finn."

The twins dashed across the street. "He scared me to death," Flossie said after they had stopped running.

"He's nuts," Freddie said. "Talking about a ghost going back to his grave."

"Maybe not," Nan said thoughtfully.

"What do you mean?" asked Bert.

"Old Ben may have seen Larry and thought he was Huck Finn," said Nan. "Larry does look like him."

"But what about the cemetery?" Bert asked. "And going back to the grave? What does that mean?"

"Don't you see?" Nan said. "That's where Larry could be hiding."

"In a graveyard?" asked Flossie.

"It's the perfect place," said Bert. He looked at his watch. "I'd like to check it out, but it's getting late. We need to check in with Mom and Dad."

The twins headed back to the steamboat.

But when they arrived, Mr. and Mrs. Bobbsey were nowhere to be found.

"They're probably visiting in somebody's cabin," said Nan.

"Well, we can't wait around forever," Bert said. "I say we go back."

"I agree with Bert," said Freddie.

"We'll need a flashlight," said Flossie, looking up at the sky. Clouds had covered the sun. "It's getting dark out there!"

Bert ran to his room. He was back in a few minutes with his Rex Sleuther flashlight. The twins ran down the gangplank and back into town.

By the time they reached the church, dark clouds had blanketed the sky. It seemed more like dusk than daytime. Huge old trees cast strangely shaped shadows on the brick church.

"I hope it doesn't rain," Nan said. She turned on the flashlight.

"Let me hold it, Nan," said Freddie.

Nan handed him the flashlight. He pointed it down at the path that led to the cemetery. The twins began to walk down the path.

All of a sudden the light went out.

"No! No!" Freddie screamed. "Stop! Stop!" A gurgling sound came from his throat.

The twins looked around anxiously.

"Freddie! Freddie!" Flossie shouted. "Where are you? Are you all right?"

The light came on. Freddie stepped out from behind a tree and burst out laughing.

"Very funny, Freddie," Nan said angrily.

"Better give me the flashlight," said Bert.

"Oh, all right," Freddie grumbled. He handed Bert the flashlight. "Can't anybody around here take a joke?"

"Some joke!" said Flossie.

The twins crept up the path toward the iron fence which enclosed the cemetery. Streaks of lightning lit up the sky. Claps of thunder boomed. Clouds raced by.

"You'd think they were making a horror movie here," said Nan. The wind tore at her brown hair. "What else is going to happen?"

A chilling, high-pitched scream pierced the air. Then something came hurtling out of the darkness—right at them!

Flossie screamed as the black shape swooped down and vanished into the trees.

"It's a nighthawk," said Bert.

Flossie gulped. "I knew it was a dumb old bird," she said.

"Sure, you did. That's why you screamed your head off," said Freddie.

"Come on." Bert cut them off. "Let's get this over with."

The lightning flashed again, followed by a clap of thunder. Bert opened the creaking iron gate. Nan and the twins followed him into the cemetery. He shone the light on the center path, lined with huge old trees. "This way," he said.

"Oh, yuck," Flossie said. "I ran into a cobweb. Help me! I can't get it off!"

Bert turned the light on Flossie, while Nan pulled the cobweb off her sister's hair.

"This is awful," Flossie said. "Is Larry worth all this trouble?"

"That's a terrible thing to say," said Nan.

Flossie stuck out her lower lip. "Well, I'm the one who got attacked by the cobweb."

"Just look at all those old tombs," said Freddie. "They look like small houses!"

"*Haunted* houses," said Flossie.

"What was that noise?" Bert asked suddenly.

Everybody stopped and listened.

"It was just the wind," Nan said. "I think that storm's about to hit."

"It sounded like that creaking gate to me," said Flossie.

"Maybe somebody's come into the cemetery," said Freddie. "Maybe they're out to get us!"

Another lightning flash lit up the sky.

"Uh, uh," said Flossie. "Something's touching my arm . . . *aaaggghhh!*" Her scream was drowned out by a clap of thunder.

Bert shone the flashlight on Flossie. "Larry!" he shouted.

Larry was crouched behind a tomb near Flossie. "Get that light out of my eyes!" he said, standing up.

"Why did you do that?" Flossie demanded. "You scared me!"

"Look who's complaining," Larry said. "What are you guys doing here? And making all that noise. It's a wonder you didn't wake up the dead!"

"Don't say that," said Nan, shuddering.

Just then it began to rain—hard.

"Oh, no," said Bert. He looked around. "We're going to get soaked if we don't find someplace to wait out the storm."

"Get in there," said Larry. He pointed at the tomb.

"I'm not going inside that thing!" said Flossie, shrinking back against Bert.

"Then stay out and get wet," Larry answered as he headed into the tomb.

"Get inside, everybody," Bert said. "Then we'll decide what we're going to do."

The five of them crowded into the tomb.

"I'm wet," said Flossie. Her voice was shaking.

Nan reached out for her sister. "Here," she said. "Get close to me and we'll keep warm."

The rain pelted the ground. Above them, lightning flashed and thunder boomed.

"Why are you hiding in the cemetery?" Freddie asked Larry.

"Because I thought nobody would look for me here," Larry answered. He looked at the Bobbseys. "But I guess I was wrong."

"You can't hide out for the rest of your life," said Bert.

Larry crawled away from the door of the tomb. "I can if I have to!" he snapped, glaring at the twins. Then he added, "I'm sorry. I know you guys are trying to help. Have you found anything to prove I didn't steal that book? I'm in real trouble!"

"We're trying," said Bert.

"But you've got to help us," Nan said. Her voice was full of concern.

Larry nodded. "There is one thing I'd forgotten," he said.

"What?" Freddie asked.

"Remember when the captain said he found my knife in the library?" Larry said. "I didn't have it in there. I dropped it in Barton Ford's room when I took his notes."

"Are you sure?" Bert asked.

A blinding light suddenly filled the tomb.

"Let's get out of here!" screamed Larry. He ran for the door. So did the Bobbseys.

They bumped into one another and Flossie fell down.

"Hey!" called a voice. "It's only me. Don't be afraid!"

"Who's *me?*" called Freddie, as he helped Flossie up.

A figure crouched in the doorway of the tomb and shone a light on his face.

"Mr. Ford!" said Flossie, rubbing her knee.

"What are you doing here?" said Bert.

"Did you follow us?" asked Nan.

"Yes, I did," said Mr. Ford.

"Why?" Bert wanted to know.

"It's very simple," Mr. Ford said. "I hoped you'd lead me to Larry. He still has that paper he stole from me!" He shone the light on Larry's face.

Mr. Ford's eyes and voice were hard. "And he's going to give it back to me," he said, stepping into the tomb. "Right now!"

8

Barton Ford's Secret

The Bobbseys and Larry drew close together as Mr. Ford bent over and entered the tomb.

"I want that paper," said Mr. Ford, straightening up. He looked at Larry. "Where is it?"

"It's hidden," said Larry.

Mr. Ford sighed. "All right," he said. "I guess I'm going to have to tell you the whole story."

"That would help," said Nan.

"I'm not writing a book," said Mr. Ford.

"Then what *are* you doing?" asked Flossie.

"I'm a special investigator with the state police," explained Mr. Ford.

"Really?" Larry asked.

"We had a tip," Mr. Ford said. "We heard that somebody would try to steal one of the rare books from the *Mississippi Princess.* A ring of thieves has been stealing valuable books and selling them to collectors."

"So you don't think that Larry stole that book?" asked Flossie.

Mr. Ford looked at Larry. "I'm not sure," he said. "Did you?"

"I told you I didn't," Larry said. "Honest!"

"Okay, I believe you," said Mr. Ford. "I came on strong against you to throw off the real thief. You know, make him careless."

"That's smart," Flossie said in an admiring voice.

"Do you have any idea who might have stolen the book?" asked Bert.

"A lot of people would do anything for $50,000," said Mr. Ford. "I need that paper back from Larry because I made notes on it about my suspects. As long as he has those notes, he's in danger!"

"Oh, Larry," Flossie said. "Give it back!"

"I don't have it," Larry insisted. "I told you, I hid it."

"Where?" Mr. Ford asked.

"On the boat," said Larry.

"Let's go back and get this straightened out," Bert said. "Mr. Ford, I think you need to explain to Captain Collins and the police what's going on, too."

"I can't do that," said Mr. Ford. "And I have to swear all of you to secrecy. If the thieves find out that you know all this, you won't be safe. No, the fewer people who know what I'm doing, the better."

"Well, all right," Nan said. "If you think that's best."

"I do," Mr. Ford said. "Come on. It's stopped raining. Let's go back to the steamboat."

Mr. Ford bent low and ducked out of the tomb. Larry and the Bobbseys followed.

"Oh, it's so muddy here," Flossie said. "It's making my shoes all gloppy."

Mr. Ford, waving his flashlight, led them down the path to the gate.

"I'm glad we're leaving," said Flossie as a flash of lightning lit up the cemetery.

"Me, too," Nan said, raising her voice over a clap of thunder. "This place is creepy."

"I still don't understand why you hid in a cemetery, Larry," Flossie said. "It's so . . . Hey, where is he, anyway?"

Mr. Ford and Bert shone their flashlights around the area.

"I can't believe this," Mr. Ford said. "He's disappeared again!"

"Look! Over there!" shouted Nan, pointing down at the ground by the fence.

Bert shone his flashlight along the iron fence.

"Those must be Larry's tracks!" said Nan.

"Come on!" shouted Mr. Ford. "After him!"

They followed Larry's tracks alongside the fence. The lightning and thunder had stopped suddenly, but the sky was still filled with dark clouds.

"He's heading toward the edge of the bluff," Bert said finally. "Where is he going?"

"Wherever it is," Nan said, "I'm not sure we'll be able to follow him."

They had reached the edge of the bluff. Bert and Mr. Ford shone their flashlights toward the river.

"It's steep," Freddie said, "but I think we can make it." He sat down and swung his legs over the side of the bluff.

"Be careful, Freddie!" said Nan.

"Do you see his tracks?" asked Mr. Ford.

"Shine the light down here," said Freddie.

"Look!" Bert said. "In the mud. He went down this way all right."

"Well, I say we go down," said Mr. Ford.

With Freddie leading the way, the others climbed down the bluff.

"The dirt is awfully loose here," Freddie said. "Watch your step."

"I'm getting mud underneath my finger-nails," complained Flossie.

"Watch it," cried Nan. "You stepped on my foot."

"Sorry," said Bert.

"How're you doing, Freddie?" Mr. Ford asked.

"I think I'm getting close to the bottom," Freddie said. "Yeah, I'm down."

Finally, the other twins and Mr. Ford reached the bottom. A moment later, they were on a narrow beach facing the river.

"Look, here are Larry's tracks!" Flossie shouted, pointing down at the wet sand.

"Come on," said Mr. Ford.

"Wait a minute," Freddie said. "Shine the light over there."

Bert shone his flashlight where Freddie was pointing.

"A cave!" said Bert.

They all rushed up to a small opening in the bluff.

"I'll bet he went in here," Freddie said. "That's where the tracks lead."

"Remember that cave where Larry said his mother hid the buried treasure?" Flossie asked. "This must be it!"

"I told you that he was just making that up," said Nan.

"No, he wasn't!" Flossie insisted stubbornly.

"That opening's pretty small," said Mr.

Ford. "Do you think Larry could have gotten through it?"

"The opening looks big enough for a kid," Freddie said. "But what about the cave?"

"Good question," said Bert. He dropped to his knees and shone his flashlight inside the cave. "The cave is bigger than it looks," he reported.

"Can we get inside?" asked Freddie.

"Well, *we* can," Bert said, "But Mr. Ford'll have to stay out here."

"That's all right," said Mr. Ford. "I'll keep watch."

"I don't want to go into that cave," said Flossie.

"Chicken!" said Freddie. Flossie shrugged.

"I don't know if this is a good idea," Nan said. "This cave looks like it's going to cave in any minute."

"It seems pretty sturdy to me," said Bert. He crawled into the cave. The other Bobbseys followed. They had to squeeze and squirm to get through the opening. But finally they made it.

"Wait there!" Bert shouted to Mr. Ford.

"Don't worry," Mr. Ford called back. "Just find Larry!"

Bert stood up and shone his flashlight around the cave. "Not too bad," he said. "Let's go!"

The twins started walking toward the rear of the cave.

"Larry!" shouted Flossie. Her voice echoed off the walls.

Suddenly the echo was drowned out by a loud flutter of wings. Moments later, bats began flying all around them.

"Let's get out of here!" cried Bert.

"Duck!" screamed Nan. "They're coming toward us!"

"Head for the entrance!" shouted Bert.

The twins covered their heads and ran. The bats were ahead of them now, flying out of the cave.

The Bobbseys had almost reached the mouth of the cave when they heard a loud rumble. Dust filled the air.

"The entrance! It caved in," Bert shouted.

"Oh, no!" cried Flossie. "We're trapped!"

9

Rowing Toward Danger

"Help!" Nan shouted.

"We've got to scream louder if we want Mr. Ford to hear us!" said Bert.

"HELP!" the Bobbseys yelled together. "HELP!"

"I don't know if he heard us," Nan said. "There's too much dirt and stuff covering the entrance."

"We'll never get out," Flossie said. "We'll be here forever!"

"No, we won't," said Bert. He shone his flashlight around the cave. "Those were Larry's tracks leading in here. I know they were. And you don't see him around, do you?"

The other Bobbseys shook their heads.

"If he were still in this cave," continued Bert, "he'd have heard us calling."

"But he didn't," said Nan. "So that means he left by another way."

"Right," said Freddie. "But *which* way?"

Bert began running to the rear of the cave.

"Don't go so fast," Flossie said. "I can't see where I'm going. Here, shine the light over here."

Bert slowed down to let the others catch up. Then he shone the light from one side of the cave to the other.

"We're going uphill," Nan said.

"And the cave's getting narrower, too," said Freddie. "I keep bumping into the wall."

"I'll bet that means we're heading for an exit," Bert said. "Come on."

"Don't rush us, Bert," Nan said. "We have to be careful. I don't want to wake up any more bats."

"Don't mention bats," Flossie said, shuddering.

"Wait a minute," Nan said suddenly.

Bert stopped walking. "What's wrong?" he asked his sister.

"I thought I saw something," Nan said. "Shine the light over there."

Bert pointed the light toward the left wall.

"There!" Nan said. "It looks like a piece of paper." She went over and picked it up. "Hold the light steady, Bert." Nan examined the paper. "This is the paper that Larry stole from Mr. Ford," she said. "That's proof that he was here."

"I'll bet he had it on him all the time," said Flossie.

"I wonder why he left it here?" said Freddie.

"Maybe he thought nobody would find it," said Flossie.

"Well, I'm taking it with me," Nan said. "Come on. There *must* be a way out of here."

The twins kept on walking through the cave. The path got steeper and narrower. Soon they had to walk single file.

"Look!" said Bert. "There's an opening. I can see some clouds. And look at these rocks. They're wet where it must have rained in. We'll have to climb up the rocks to get out of here."

The twins started climbing. Finally, they stood in the fresh, damp night air. They were back in the cemetery at the top of the bluff.

Freddie ran to the edge. "Here, let me have the flashlight." He took it from Bert and shone it downward toward the beach by the river. "There's where we were. But where's Mr. Ford?"

"Maybe he went for help," Nan said. "He's not on the beach."

"Come on," Bert said. "It looks like it's going to start pouring again any minute. We need to get back to the *Princess*."

When they got back to the boat, the twins headed for the Orleans Room.

"We look terrible," Nan said as they stood outside the restaurant. "We're all muddy."

"We've got to find Mom and Dad," Bert said. "I just hope they won't be too mad at us."

Just then, they saw Mr. Ford come out of the Orleans Room. He was talking to Captain Collins. He stopped when he saw the Bobbseys and his mouth dropped open. He rushed up to them.

"Are you kids all right?" he asked anxiously.

"Why didn't you help us?" Flossie asked.

"I came back for help," Mr. Ford said. "How'd you get out? And where's Larry?"

The captain looked at Mr. Ford. "What's this?" he asked. "You mean you found Larry and you let him get away?"

"Well, I . . ." stammered Mr. Ford.

"*We* found him first," Flossie said. "But we lost him."

"That kid is nothing but trouble," Captain

Collins said, slamming his hand flat against the rail. "Well, I'll put some men on guard at the gangplank. They'll spot him if he tries to sneak back aboard. And the rest of the crew will go searching in the morning. As for me, I'm going to bed." He walked away.

Mr. Ford turned to the twins. "Listen, kids," he whispered. "I really was trying to get help. But I couldn't say anything in front of Captain Collins. Remember, nobody else is supposed to know what I'm really doing."

"Oh, okay," Bert said with a sigh. They were all too tired to argue.

"I'll see you in the morning," said Mr. Ford. "Then we'll decide what to do." He turned and headed down the deck.

"Where in the world have you been?"

The twins looked up. Mr. and Mrs. Bobbsey were staring at them.

"I can explain everything," said Bert.

"I certainly hope you can," said Mr. Bobbsey sternly. "And your explanation is going to start *right now.*"

"Let's get you some dinner first," Mrs. Bobbsey said. She led the family down to the ship's coffee shop. The twins were in no shape to eat in the Orleans Room.

Mr. Bobbsey ordered food for the children and coffee for himself and Mrs. Bobbsey.

"Okay, let's hear about it," he said to Bert. "We were worried sick about you."

"We were only trying to find Larry," Bert said when he'd finished the story. "Or we'd never have gone into that cave."

"That doesn't matter," Mr. Bobbsey said. "You could have been hurt!"

"I'm sorry, Dad," said Flossie.

"Me, too," Freddie said. Nan nodded.

"Where do you think Larry is now?" asked Mrs. Bobbsey.

"Who knows?" asked Freddie, popping his last french fry into his mouth.

"Well, I know it's time for bed," said Mr. Bobbsey. "So all of you had better take showers. Then get some sleep. We'll talk in the morning."

The next morning, Bert and Freddie were awakened by noises on deck. They dressed quickly and rushed out of their cabin.

Flossie and Nan were already in the corridor, waiting for them.

"Looks like trouble up on the Sun Deck," Nan said. "Let's go see."

When they reached the Sun Deck, they saw several members of the crew heading for the wheelhouse.

"What's happening?" Bert shouted to one of the crew members.

"Somebody's ruined one of the engines," said the man. "This boat's not going anywhere until we get it fixed."

"Isn't the crew going out to look for Larry?" asked Nan.

"That'll have to wait," said the man. "Captain Collins wants the engine fixed first." He turned and went into the wheelhouse.

"This looks pretty suspicious to me," Nan said. "Now nobody can go looking for Larry except for us—and Mr. Ford."

"You know," Flossie said, "he doesn't seem like a very good police officer to me."

"You're right," Bert agreed. "We're the ones who found Larry. And Mr. Ford wasn't much help when we were trapped in the cave."

"I sure wouldn't want him looking for me," said Freddie.

"That reminds me." Nan took the paper she'd found in the cave out of her jacket pocket. "I forgot about this." She opened it up. "I guess we should give it back to Mr. Ford. After all, it does belong to him." She looked at the paper for a moment. Then her eyes lit up. "Hey, look at this!" she said excitedly.

The other twins gathered around Nan.

"What's wrong?" asked Freddie.

"This all makes sense now," Nan said. "Look!"

The twins studied the writing on the paper: 50,000. AUTO AHF PAC, 11223 21st, NO. 555-7906.

"It still looks like a bunch of numbers and letters to me," Flossie said, frowning.

"Look closer," Nan said. "Don't you see?"

"Nope," said Flossie.

"Me neither," said Freddie, shaking his head.

"Wait a minute," Bert said. "I'm beginning to get it." He looked at the other twins. "Mr. Ford said this information was about somebody who had stolen that rare book. But it's not!"

"That's right," Nan said with a nod. "It's about somebody who wants to *buy* it!"

"How come?" asked Flossie.

"What do all the numbers and letters *mean?*" asked Freddie.

"Remember when Mr. Ford first accused Larry of stealing that book?" Nan asked. "He said it was worth $50,000. That's what this 50,000 must mean."

"Then these next letters must stand for: Autographed *Adventures of Huckleberry Finn,*" said Bert. "See?"

"Oh, yeah," Freddie said. "I get it."

"But what about the rest of it?" Flossie asked. "What does PAC mean?"

"PAC might be the initials of the person who wants to buy it," Nan said. "And I'm positive the buyer's address is 11223 21st Street in NO— New Orleans. And the buyer's telephone number is 555-7906!"

"That means that Mr. Ford isn't a special investigator with the state police," Bert said. "He's planning to sell the book to this PAC when we get to New Orleans!"

"That's it!" said Flossie.

"I'd like to see Mr. Ford explain all this away," said Nan.

"We need to find Captain Collins first," Bert said. "As ship's captain, he has the power to arrest Mr. Ford."

The twins rushed off to look for the captain. They found him in the engine room, overseeing the repairs to the damaged engine.

"I haven't seen Mr. Ford this morning," Captain Collins said when the twins asked him.

"We need to find him," Bert said. "We think he's the one who—"

"Kids! Kids!" the captain interrupted. "I can't talk to you now. I'm busy." He turned to a crew member. "You need to get another part from the supply room."

The twins followed the crew member out of the engine room.

"I saw Mr. Ford," the crew member told them. "Early this morning. He was leaving the boat. But I haven't seen him since." The man hurried off.

"He's going to look for Larry!" said Nan.

"We've got to find Larry first," Bert said. "If we don't, there's no telling what will happen to him!"

The twins hurried to the gangplank.

But when they got there, Nan said, "Wait a minute. We can't just rush off the boat without a plan. We have to think! Where would Larry have gone?"

"Maybe he went back to the cemetery," suggested Flossie.

"No," Bert said, shaking his head. "He'd know that Mr. Ford might look for him there. I'm sure he's someplace else now."

"But *where?*" asked Freddie.

"Just let me think," Bert said. "Maybe I should go get my copy of *The Adventures of Huckleberry Finn* and start looking through it."

"There's no time," Nan said. "Just try to remember some other places where Huck hid."

"Well . . ." Bert began. He looked out over

the river. Suddenly his eyes lit up. "That's it!" he said.

"What?" asked Flossie.

"See those two little islands in the middle of the river?" Bert asked. "Huck Finn and his friend Jim hid together on an island once. I'll bet that's where Larry is now!"

"Oh, great," Nan said. "How do you plan for us to get over there? Swim?"

"We'll borrow a rowboat," Bert said. "I saw some tied up at the dock. Come on, let's get some life jackets."

A short while later, the twins found a rowboat tied up near the *Princess*.

"I hope the owner doesn't mind if we borrow this," Bert said as he untied the rope that moored the boat.

"It's for a good cause," said Nan.

The twins stepped carefully into the rowboat. Bert and Nan each grabbed an oar and pushed the boat away from the dock into the river.

They rowed steadily toward the islands.

"How would Larry have gotten over there?" asked Flossie.

"He'd have done the same thing we're doing," Bert said. "Or floated across on a log. Remember, he's just like Huck Finn. So he'd know what to do."

"Well, *we'd* better think of something to do right now," Freddie said, "because somebody's coming after us."

Nan and Bert turned and looked toward the shore. A familiar figure was getting into a rowboat. He grabbed the oars and began to row.

"That's Mr. Ford!" exclaimed Nan. "He looks angry. And he's headed straight toward us!"

10

Catching a Crook

"Row faster, Nan!" Bert shouted.

They began rowing as fast as they could.

"Look!" said Freddie. "There's a rowboat tied up at the first island. It's hidden under some brush, but I can see part of it."

"Head that way, Nan!" shouted Bert.

"Mr. Ford's gaining on us!" cried Flossie.

The twins rowed faster.

The rowboat finally hit the island. Bert jumped out and pulled the boat up on shore.

The other twins got out of the boat and followed Bert into the brush.

"Larry!" cried Nan.

Suddenly Larry stepped out of some brush into view. "How'd you find me?" he asked.

"There's no time to explain," Bert said. "Mr. Ford's after us. He's the thief, and we can prove it. Come on!"

Larry hesitated a second. Then he ran after the twins, toward the rowboat they'd borrowed. Bert pushed the boat into the water, and they jumped in. Mr. Ford was only a few feet from them.

Bert and Nan rowed hard, away from the island.

Mr. Ford made an abrupt turn and started toward them. His face was red with anger and he was rowing as hard as he could.

"He's gaining on us!" shouted Nan.

The twins rowed harder. But it was no use.

"There's too much weight in our boat!" cried Bert.

Mr. Ford rammed their boat with his, almost causing them to tip over.

He stood up and grabbed for Larry. But he missed. "You're not going to cause me any more trouble!" he shouted. He aimed an oar at Bert. But Bert grabbed Mr. Ford's boat and shoved with all his strength.

Mr. Ford lost his balance and toppled into the river.

"Look!" Flossie cried. "A speedboat is coming toward us!"

"It's Captain Collins!" Nan yelled. She looked at Larry. "And . . . your dad!"

Larry had a smile on his face. "For once I'm going to be glad to see him."

Mr. Ford was holding on to the side of his rowboat when the captain and his crew arrived.

"Would anyone care to explain this?" Captain Collins asked when one of the crew had cut the speedboat's engine.

"Glad to," Bert said. "Mr. Ford stole the book from the library and tried to blame Larry. He's the one who put Larry's knife by the display case."

"You're sure about all this?" asked Captain Collins.

"Positive," Nan said. "Look in that knapsack in Mr. Ford's rowboat. I'll bet you'll find the missing book. He was probably planning to leave the *Mississippi Princess* today."

Mr. Ford pulled himself up and reached for the knapsack. But Captain Collins beat him to it. The captain opened the sack and smiled. "Guess what I just found?" he asked, holding up the book.

"All right!" said Larry and the Bobbseys.

"We even have the address and telephone number of the person in New Orleans that Mr.

Ford was going to sell the book to," Nan said. She gave Captain Collins the paper Larry had stolen from Mr. Ford.

"The police will be very interested in that," said Captain Collins. He and Mr. Granville each grabbed one of Mr. Ford's wrists and lifted him out of the water into the speedboat. Captain Collins looked at Mr. Ford's hands.

"How did your hands get so greasy?" he asked Mr. Ford. "Wrecking my engine?"

Mr. Ford didn't say anything, but his face was pale.

Mr. Granville hugged Larry. "You all right, son?"

"Sure," said Larry. He smiled. "I'm okay, Dad."

"This is one time we all owe Larry an apology," said Captain Collins.

"I accept," Larry said.

The twins grinned.

"Well, come on then," said Captain Collins. "The crew has finished repairing the engine. We're ready to cruise on down the Mississippi—just as soon as we turn Mr. Ford over to the police."

Mr. Ford stared down at the floor of the speedboat, his head in his hands.

Bert tied Mr. Ford's rowboat to the captain's speedboat. Then he and Nan followed Captain

Collins back toward the *Mississippi Princess*.

Flossie moved next to Larry. "When are you going to tell me where that hidden treasure is?"

Larry opened his eyes wide. "What treasure?" he asked.

"The one you said your mother hid in a cave for you," said Flossie.

"Oh, *that*. I was just making that up," Larry said. "Don't tell me you believed it!" He grinned from ear to ear.

Everybody laughed—except Flossie.

"You know, Larry, maybe you should give up acting like Huck Finn," Bert said. "You make up so many stories, you'd be a better Mark Twain!"

"I wouldn't mind being famous," Larry said, smiling. "Even if it's just for getting into trouble!"